"Perkins!" Lexie cried, [...] [...]
edged my way into the room. "I'm going to
paint the best picture of you ever. And Jess is
going to help me."

Jess said: "You'll like having your portrait
done, won't you, Perkins? If we win, your
picture will be in the paper. It's going to be
brilliant."

"And," Lexie said, "we're not going to do
the normal cat-things. We're not going to
show you sleeping, or looking cute or
anything. It's going to be dead unusual."

I have never thought of myself as cute,
but I did not say anything. . .

Picasso Perkins is the second title in a series
about a group of cats who are good friends,
the Cats of Cuckoo Square.

PICASSO
PERKINS

For Nicholas West

PICASSO PERKINS
A YOUNG CORGI BOOK: 0 552 54555 4

First publication in Great Britain

PRINTING HISTORY
Young Corgi edition published 1997

3 5 7 9 10 8 6 4 2

Set in 17/21pt Bembo Schoolbook
by Phoenix Typesetting, Ilkley, West Yorkshire

Young Corgi Books are published by Transworld Publishers Ltd,
61–63 Uxbridge Road, London W5 5SA,
in Australia by Transworld Publishers,
c/o Random House Australia Pty Ltd,
20 Alfred Street, Milsons Point, NSW 2061,
in New Zealand by Transworld Publishers,
c/o Random House New Zealand,
18 Poland Road, Glenfield, Auckland,
and in South Africa by Transworld Publishers,
c/o Random House (Pty) Ltd,
Endulini, 5a Jubilee Road, Parktown 2193.

Made and printed in Great Britain by
Cox & Wyman Ltd, Reading, Berkshire.

THE CATS OF CUCKOO SQUARE

Picasso Perkins

ADÈLE GERAS

Illustrated by Tony Ross

YOUNG CORGI BOOKS

1. The Painting Competition

My name is Perkins and I am an old cat and a wise cat. I am, in addition, familiar with all the Sayings of Our Ancient Furry Ancestors. They say, for instance: "Breakfast is the right meal for interesting news."

Today at breakfast, Lexie said: "Guess what? There's a painting competition in the *Bugle*. It's called

'Paint Your Pet', and there are cash prizes! Also, the winning picture gets printed in the paper."

"Lovely, dear," said Melissa. "Please eat your cereal."

Lexie continued, through a spoonful of food: "Entries have to be in on Monday. I wish I'd known about this before . . . we haven't got enough time. I want to do a portrait of Perkins. Jess'll be here in a second and I'll tell her about it, and we'll do it together. It's sure to win. Perkins is so beautiful, aren't you, Perkins?"

I looked up and blinked at her to show her my gratitude. Little did I know what I was letting myself in for. Lexie likes to get her own way. She is not a calm and docile child. She goes upstairs two at a time; she never walks when she can run, and she climbs trees as well as many cats.

The "Jess" she was expecting is her best friend and she lives next door to us. Lexie is a great talker, just like her mother. Melissa is a teacher at Lexie's school, and believes in recycling and the creative use of various foodstuffs. The children in her class are forever making sculptures from old cornflakes packets and egg-boxes, and sticking lentils, beans and uncooked macaroni on to cardboard, spraying them with gold and silver paint and taking them home to proud parents.

Roland Blythe, Lexie's father, is an artist.

"I'm a pro," he says. "A real professional. There's not many who can say they make a decent living from their brushes. Starving in a garret wouldn't suit us, eh?" he says to his wife and daughter.

Nevertheless, Roland would love to have his paintings exhibited in a proper art gallery. That is what he would call success. His pictures end up on greetings cards, calendars and wrapping-paper. Still, I know he has been preparing what he calls "real pictures" in a shed at the end of the garden, which he calls "my studio". It is a delightful, warm place to curl up in during the chilly months of the year, and Roland likes to chat to me as he works.

"I value your opinion, Perkins," he says to me. "Tell me what you think of this. I call it: 'Seagulls at Sunset'." He likes painting animals and birds. He has done "Puppies at Playtime", "Fluffy Fun" (rabbits) and "Purrfect Peace" (kittens asleep). I never tell Roland my opinion of his work, but Blossom, Callie and Geejay know that I am not a great admirer of his pictures. Their colours are too bright or too pale. They are all much the same as one another and they are what Lexie and Jess call "soppy". Whenever Roland shows me something new, I purr enthusiastically and pretend to examine the painting carefully, but often my eyes are half-closed and I

am thinking about my next sleep
and where I might be most
comfortable. I would not wish to
hurt his feelings, for as the Furry
Ancestors say: "A purring cat is
never short of minced chicken liver."
But let me return to the breakfast
table. Lexie had decided my portrait
was going to win a prize.

"That's very exciting, Lexie," said
Roland, "but I have some thrilling
news of my own. Look at this letter."

He waved it around, narrowly
missing the milk jug. "Wilfred de
Crespay is coming to view my work
on Saturday. That's tomorrow . . .
oh, my word!" He began to fan
himself with the letter. "I've gone
quite hot and bothered."

"Who's Wilfred the Crispy?" Lexie
said. "Is he foreign?"

16

"De Crespay," said Roland. "His name is probably of Norman origin, but he is English. He is one of the best-known art-dealers in town. He goes to see what artists are painting and chooses pictures to go in his gallery. Then rich people buy them for lots and lots of money. I could be famous! I wrote to him some time ago, but never really expected an answer . . . Goodness me! And such short notice! He says he likes to catch painters as they are, and not give them too much time to prepare new work. But I must go and begin to get everything into a fit state to be seen."

When Roland is arranging paintings, it is as well to avoid his studio. He picks things up and puts them down somewhere else. He takes three steps backwards to look at something and if I happen to be in the way, my tail is almost certainly trodden on. So I decided to settle down in Lexie's room. Lexie is an excellent child in many ways, but no-one would call her tidy. Her bedroom looks as though a medium-sized hurricane has lifted every garment, every book and every knick-knack, whirled them about in the air for a time and put them down in unexpected places.

It is quite normal to
find a trainer on
the window-sill,

or a book on the pillow,

or a pair of socks
draped over the
dressing-table mirror.
Still, she is always glad to see me,
and there is generally a space on
the bed into which I can fit
myself if I curl up really small.
Sometimes good luck is with me,
and one of Lexie's cardigans is
spread out and waiting for me.

"Perkins!" she cried, following me
as I edged my way into the room.
"I'm going to paint the best picture
of you ever. And Jess is going to help
me."

Jess had already arrived at our
house, waiting to walk to school
with Lexie. She said: "You'll like
having your portrait done, won't
you, Perkins? If we win, your picture
will be in the paper. It's going to be
brilliant."

"And," Lexie said, "we're not going to do the normal cat-things. We're not going to show you sleeping, or looking cute or anything. It's going to be dead unusual."

I have never thought of myself as cute, but I did not say anything.

"We'll think," Lexie continued, "of good places for you to sit."

"Or stand," said Jess.

"Or maybe lie," said Lexie. "You'll have to keep very still. You can do that, can't you, Perkins? You're often still for ages, just staring into space."

I jumped on to Lexie's bed and decided to ignore her last remark. Many humans think that cats stare

into space, but we do not. We are
thinking cat-thoughts (for example:
do the sounds from the kitchen mean
that Melissa is cooking, and if she is,
will there be scraps for me?),
dreaming cat-dreams and seeing cat-
things invisible to the human eye,
such as specks of flying dust drifting
through the air and catching the
light.

"We'll use pastel crayons," said Lexie.

"No, water-colours," said Jess. "I want to use my new paint-box."

"OK," said Lexie. "We'll try water-colours, but maybe we should do some sketches first. There's a few minutes before we have to go to school. My dad always does sketches."

It occurred to me that sketching had not done much to improve Roland's pictures, but I kept quiet and hoped the girls would be content to draw me as I lay on the bed.

Not a bit of it. Lexie picked me up, and said: "Now, stand here, Perkins, and try to look fierce!"

She deposited me on top of the

bookshelf and fierce is just what I felt, so I glowered at her. The Furry Ancestors say: "Better wide awake than being woken up," and it is true that I intensely dislike being interrupted as I am falling asleep, so I went on glowering.

"That's lovely!" Lexie squeaked. "Now don't move while we draw you."

She and Jess began to scratch around on sheets of paper. The top of the bookshelf was covered with bits and pieces: jewellery, pencils, ornaments and so forth, and there wasn't an inch of space where a cat could put his feet. So I jumped down on to the carpet, and ran out of the room.

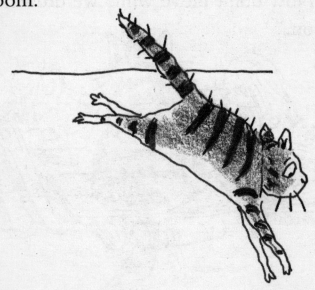

"Perkins!" Lexie shouted. "Come back here at once! Naughty cat!"

She tore down the stairs behind me, and very nearly caught me, but even at my advanced age, I am quite nippy on my feet in an emergency, and thankfully, Lexie cannot follow me through the cat-flap. I made my way to the garden in the middle of the Square.

2. Hiding from Lexie

"Please do not let her find me," I said to my friends. "I am staying here under this bush and I am not coming out till Lexie and Jess have left for school."

The other Cuckoo Square cats stared at me in some amazement. If there is one thing they all know, it is how fond I am of Lexie and how devoted she is to me.

I am the oldest cat in the Square. I came here with Roland and Melissa Blythe when they first moved into number 27, thirteen years ago. In those days I was a sweet, fluffy kitten and so good-tempered and loving that I was called Purrkins. But the Furry Ancestors say: "The name must grow with the cat," so I have become Perkins. Lexie's real name is Alexandra. She is eight years old.

My closest companions among the
neighbourhood cats are Blossom,

Callie

and Geejay.
They look up to me and I find that
I can often give them good advice.
I enjoy sitting with them in the
little garden in the middle of
Cuckoo Square. We tell one

another stories about the humans
who feed and shelter us and amuse
us greatly with their strange
behaviour.

"Your family," Callie said to me
one day, "is stranger than most."

"That's because," said Blossom,
"Mr Blythe is an Artist. It's a well-
known fact that artistic people are
not like everyone else. For one thing
they wear funny clothes. Think of
Mr Blythe's beret."

This is made of
black velvet, and
we cats smile
every time
we see it.

"He calls it his Rembrandt beret," I told my friends. "Rembrandt was a famous artist who lived long ago."

"Is Mr Blythe famous?" Geejay wanted to know.

"Not really," I told them, "though he would love to be."

I am grateful that I do not have to wear strange garments. I am proud of the glossiness of my tabby fur, of the youthful sparkle in my amber eyes, and of my imposing size, but I am a modest cat, so I try never to mention these things.

"Look!" said Callie. "There's Lexie going off to school with Jess."

"They are never apart," I told her. "Any room that Lexie is in will contain Jess and vice versa. And

now, they will be spending most of the time in our house, because of me. They are after me. That is why I am hiding. Lexie was going to start the project that very minute."

"What project, Perkins?" Geejay asked. "All we know is that Lexie is after you, but we don't know why."

"Did I not mention why?"

"No," said Blossom. "You didn't."

33

"Lexie is going to paint my portrait. There is a competition in the newspaper, and she intends to win it. She has just tried to get me to stand very still exactly where she wants me and it was most uncomfortable, I can tell you. I would much rather it did not happen again, and therefore I have decided to hide in the Square when she is at home. If she cannot find me, then she will not be able to pull me about this way and that. While Lexie is at school, I shall be warm and comfortable in the house, and when she returns I shall come out here."

"But it's getting so cold here in the evenings," said Callie. "And the bangs have started. I heard some last night."

We all shuddered. Every leaf on the trees in the Square was turning red or gold or brown and spiralling down to make a wonderfully crackly sitting-spot for us cats, but November meant Firework Night, and hiding in the darkest spaces we could find until the fizzings and the whizzings of a thousand exploding missiles were over.

The Furry Ancestors say: "When fire leaps in the sky, sensible cats hide in the nearest cupboard."

"I shall be brave," I said. "It is only for a few days. The entries for the competition have to be in on Monday, and today is Friday. I will say goodbye to you all now, and go in for a sleep on my special shawl. Have I told you that Melissa has put out a beautifully striped, soft, hand-knitted shawl just for me?"

"Often," said Geejay. "You've often told us."

I miaowed a farewell to my friends and made my way home. I pushed myself through the cat-flap – a tight fit these days – and into the kitchen.

3. Posing for the Portrait

I looked all round the kitchen to make sure Roland was not in there, using his horrible hissing coffee machine to make himself a drink. A blissful silence filled every corner of the room. I jumped on to my special chair, and began my morning wash. First, I cleaned my face, then I licked my front paws and then I tackled the

hard-to-reach bit of my back,
thinking what a fortunate feline I
was to have such a beautifully soft,
stripy shawl to lie on. Then I put my
face between my paws and fell into
a deep slumber. I do not know how
long I had been sleeping when I
heard the sound of a key opening
the front door.

"Coo-ee!" called Melissa.
"Roland, dear, are you there?"

"Dad!" shouted Lexie. "It's us.
Where are you?"

"I was in the box-room a moment ago," said Roland. "I was looking for some frames. I've nearly decided what to show Mr de Crespay tomorrow. What are you doing here?"

"We've been sent home from school," said Lexie. "The boiler's broken and it won't be fixed till after the weekend. Isn't that ace?" She was bouncing up and down. "Jess is coming over," she continued, "and we'll do the portrait. We can spend all day on it, can't we, Perkins?"

I had tucked my head firmly under my paws and was busily pretending to be still asleep.

Lexie was not deceived. "You're awake, Perkins," she said, stroking me. "I know you are. I can tell because your tail is twitching. And," she went on, "don't even think about running off to the Square or even the studio because I shan't let you."

She put the cat-flap cover on, and

my whiskers quivered with indignation.

"When Jess comes," she said to Melissa, "send her up to the box-room to help me bring paper down."

"How much paper are you going to need?" Melissa asked. "You can only send one picture in, you know."

"We might," said Lexie, "need a few sheets to practise on, till we get it right. That's OK, isn't it?"

"It's fine," said Melissa. "Just leave everything tidy in there, that's all."

The box-room is called that because it is full of boxes: the packets and egg-cartons and yoghurt pots and loo-paper rolls that Melissa uses to make things with her children at school. There is also a cupboard in

there where the paper lives. Melissa's brother, Uncle Don, works with a machine that spits out yards and yards of it every day. He calls the machine a computer, and he brings his sister piles and piles of clean white paper, which everyone uses for drawing and painting.

Lexie was in the box-room for a long time, and when she returned to the kitchen, she whispered to me:

"Don't say a word, Perkins, but this isn't computer-printout. I've taken some of Dad's real paper. Otherwise, the pictures are going to look babyish, don't you think?"

I thought to myself that Roland might be extremely angry when he discovered that Lexie was helping herself to his possessions, but Lexie said: "He won't even notice it's gone, he's in such a state about Wilfred the Scrumpy."

Jess arrived soon after, and then the torment began.

"Now, Perkins, stand up," said Lexie. I ignored her. She and Jess were sitting at the kitchen table. They each had a jam-jar full of water, and a paint-box in front of

them, and also a big sheet of paper
for the picture.

"He's going to be difficult," said Lexie. "I'll go and get him to stand up." She picked me up, and shook me gently. Then she put me down on all four paws. "There," she said. "Now stay like that and don't move. Try and look like a statue."

I obliged her for a moment, but I sat down on my haunches after a while.

"Perkins!" Lexie shrieked. "What are you doing? Silly cat!"

"He looks all right," said Jess. "Let's do him like that. He still looks quite fierce."

I glanced at the kitchen door and noticed that Melissa had not closed it behind her. The Furry Ancestors would have been proud of me. I recalled one of their best-known sayings: "The open door waits for the fleeing cat," and before Lexie could say "Jam-jar", I had streaked through it, and bounded upstairs.

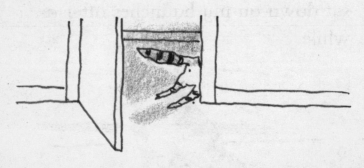

"Perkins!" I heard the girls calling after me, and soon they were thumping up the stairs behind me. I ran into Roland and Melissa's bedroom and dived under the duvet, making myself as flat as I possibly could, because everyone knows the ancient saying: "A flat cat is a safe cat, a flatter cat is a safer cat, and the flattest cat is the safest cat of all."

"I can see you," Lexie cried. "There's a big lump in the middle of the bed – that's you, Perkins, and I'm coming to get you!"

It is one thing to know a saying by heart and quite another to be able to obey it. I sighed. It was clear that I would never be nearly flat enough to escape Lexie's sharp eyes. Still, I was not going to let the girls crawl under the duvet to find me. That would have been most undignified. I made my own way out, trying to look as though I did not at all mind being found and carried back to the kitchen.

As soon as she had settled me where she thought I ought to be, Lexie shut the door very firmly and said: "Let's start again, then."

The sheets of paper fell off the table like leaves from the trees outside. The portrait would not come right.

"His head's too big," said Jess after one attempt.

"Now his paws look funny," said Lexie, throwing another sheet of paper on to the floor.

"And I don't think he should sit like that," she added, tossing the next bit of paper aside. "Let's move him."

I sighed. No sooner was I placed in one position than the girls decided they wanted me somewhere else, and they moved me around the kitchen until I felt quite dizzy. First, they put me on the dresser.

Then they put me
beside the door.

Then they tried me
on the window-sill
and the pile of rejected portraits
grew and grew until the whole
floor was covered with white,
paint-streaked sheets.

"Girls!" Melissa said when she came into the kitchen to cook the supper. "What *have* you been doing?"

"It's Perkins's fault," said Jess. "He keeps moving. We can't get it right."

"He's a cat," said Lexie. "He's never been an artist's model. He'll be better next time, now that he's used to it."

I groaned.

Melissa said: "Well, I can't have this mess everywhere. Wilfred de Crespay is coming to lunch tomorrow, and I haven't even started on the quiche."

"Wilfred the Crunchy!" said Lexie, and she and Jess began to giggle.

"Stop being silly, girls," said

Melissa, "and please take any paper you don't want to the studio, and leave it in a neat pile on the shelf there. I'll take any sheets you decide you've finished with into school when we go back. I can use it for some papier-mâché masks we're making."

Lexie and Jess, still snorting with laughter, gathered up armfuls of paper and made their way to the studio.

"Poor old Perkins," said Melissa. "Off you go to the Square, then. You've been very patient."

Geejay was the only cat I could find to talk to. He said: "Blossom and Callie have gone back to their houses. I don't suppose they will be out again tonight."

"After the afternoon I've had," I told him, "I shall make sure I spend most of this evening and tomorrow under this very bush. I have not had a moment's peace."

"Poor old you," said Geejay.

I appreciated his sympathy, and I thought I had worked out a perfect way of avoiding Lexie, but I did not know then about the storm blowing through the sky on its way towards us, which would change every one of my plans.

4. In the Studio

The storm was one of the fiercest I had ever seen. I was forced to leave the Square and come inside much earlier than I had intended, but mercifully, Lexie had already gone to sleep. Gales battered the trees and shook the windows in their frames all night long, and sleet fell from the sky like little grey needles. By the time morning came, the storm had stopped being quite so stormy, but rain was pouring down the panes of the kitchen window, and the wind was still rattling the cat-flap. This was an Indoors Day if ever there was one. Not even Geejay, who is the bravest of us all, would venture out on a morning like this.

As the Furry Ancestors say: "Warm and dry is better than wet and cold." Before the Blythes woke up, I worried about a hiding-place. Lexie knew all my secret cupboards and quiet spots and she and Jess intended to spend the morning working on their portrait of me. They had said so yesterday. It was Roland who came to my rescue.

"I've got everything set up in the studio," he announced at breakfast, "and I don't want anyone – *anyone at all*, Lexie, do you understand? – coming in there and spoiling all my hard work. I've touched up a few of the pictures, so some of the paint isn't even quite dry. Out of bounds, OK?"

"OK, Dad," said Lexie, attacking her toast with a buttery knife. "Precious Mr Wilfred the Munchy will see them all just as you've arranged them. I'm going to be busy anyway. We've got to finish our entry for the competition."

I jumped down from the chair and made my way over to the cat-flap. I would have to sneak out as quietly as I could, and then cross the muddy, dripping garden, but it would be worth it. A whole morning till lunchtime in a place that Lexie had been forbidden to visit — what could be better? I chose my moment carefully. Lexie and her mother were in the middle of a loud and extremely boring argument about whether or not Lexie needed a new pair of jeans. I edged my way over to the cat-flap, and pushed at it with my nose. A blast of icy air containing far too much wetness to be comfortable blew right up my nostrils.

"Courage, Perkins!" I said to myself. "Remember – Lexie and Jess will never find you. Onwards!"

Out into the garden I went, and I do not think I have ever crossed it so fast. Sodden leaves fluttered around my paws, sharp winds puffed at my fur, and rain seemed to be coming at me from all directions. I knew the studio would be shut, but I had my

secret door which no-one knew about. There was a small gap between the planks of one wall, right at the bottom, and I would have to squeeze through that. I remembered the saying: "The closed portal invites the furry paw," and I did it, but not without a great deal of difficulty. I am larger than I thought I was, and by the time I had found my way in, I felt as though I'd been stretched and squashed into a sort of snake-shape.

The studio was not as warm as when Roland was in it, with his heater on, but after the horrors of the garden, it seemed very pleasant. I shook myself and licked myself clean, and looked around to see where I could sleep. Roland's paintings were standing up all round the room, and the big pile of Lexie and Jess's used paper sat tidily on the first shelf. I nosed around in the corners, and by a wonderful stroke of luck I discovered in one of them an old jumper that Roland had forgotten to pick up.

"Perfect, Perkins, just the ticket!" I said, and began to settle myself in the woolly bed I had found. I suppose I must have fallen asleep at once. Running so fast first thing in the morning and then squeezing through such a tiny gap had exhausted me.

Then a particularly strong wind came along and blew the studio door open. Roland must have forgotten to lock it. It is not quite true to say I woke up. The noise was such a shock that I leapt into the air with every separate hair of my fur standing on end. The gale now blowing into the studio lifted Lexie and Jess's pieces of paper right off the shelf and spread them out all over the floor. It also knocked over a small vase of flowers that Roland was in the middle of painting, and

the water made a puddle round the
easel, which had been set up near
the window.

No sooner had the gale opened the door, than another gust appeared and slammed it shut again. I waited to see whether the wind had decided to leave the studio alone for a while, and then I went to investigate the puddle. I am very fond of puddles. Indeed, I enjoy them as much as any cat I know, and I had a lovely time for a while, dipping my paws and licking the edges of the water.

Then I did something I should never have done. I leapt up on to the shelf where Roland keeps his paints. I heard voices and took fright. I thought Lexie might be disobeying her father, and coming to find me. It turned out to be the neighbours, talking about the damage the storm had done in their garden. The shelf is narrow, and I landed very precisely on top of Roland's paint-box, which he had left open. Each of my paws was now covered with a different colour. The paint was powdery, and I disliked most intensely the way it smelled and the way it felt.

"The puddle, Perkins!" I said to myself. "Remember what the Furry

Ancestors advise: 'Paddle in a puddle for perfect paw hygiene'."

This worked well. I walked backwards and forwards across the girls' pictures lying on the floor, and my paws dried very nicely. At first I left colourful tracks on the paper, but these grew paler and paler, and at

last I considered my paws to be clean enough to lick. I was wondering whether to do them now, or wait until I had made my way back to the house, when I heard Roland's voice saying: "This way, Mr de Crespay, please follow me," and then another, higher voice saying: "Oh, do call me Wilfred, I beseech you! De Crespay is too, too formal, don't you think?"

I shot away and hid behind a rather large canvas that was leaning against one wall. The whole family had come to the studio with this distinguished visitor. I peeped out to get a good look at him. He was tall and spaghetti-thin and he wore a long purple velvet jacket and green boots.

Lexie and Jess were standing very close to me, and I could hear them whispering and trying not to giggle.

"Call me the Chewy!" Jess breathed.

"No, no," Lexie murmured. "That's too, too formal. Just Chewy, please!"

Wilfred was silent for a long time. The mess before his eyes was clearly not quite what he was expecting, but he took a deep breath and began to peer at everything. Then he sighed. Roland followed him about anxiously, also somewhat puzzled at the state of his studio. Melissa was frowning. She could see that Roland was worried. The famous art-dealer hummed to himself. Then he bent

down and began to pick up all the sheets of paper I had walked over.

"This," he said. "This is very different from most of your work, Roland. Perhaps it's a new departure, and I must say, I am somewhat dazzled by its sheer beauty and elegance. Look at these delicate traceries of colour! Look at the truth of the line – oh, it's in the spirit of the great Japanese Masters – you really have Found Yourself, dear chap, haven't you? The Americans will be thrilled to ribbons, trust me, my dear – yes, yes, I think we will all, in the words of someone or other, clean up, and laugh all the way to the bank!"

"But," said Roland, blushing, "Mr de Crespay . . ."

"Wilfred," said Wilfred, "I implore you!"

"Sorry . . . Wilfred . . . well, these are not my work."

"Not your work? Whatever can you mean? You don't suppose . . ." He looked at Lexie and Jess and winked at them. "You don't suppose he has an army of elves that comes and paints these masterpieces while he's asleep, do you?"

"No," said Lexie. "He doesn't. Those look a bit like the pictures Jess and I did this morning. This is Jess." She pushed Jess forward. "But ours didn't have those coloured bits there. I don't know how those could

possibly have got there."

Wilfred looked at the girls, then
back at the paintings. "Extraordinary
. . . I don't know what to call them
. . . They are VISIONS!"

"They weren't meant to be
visions," said Lexie. "They're
supposed to be portraits of Perkins.
Perkins is our cat."

"Well, I'm lost for words!" said Wilfred. "I don't know when I've seen such work, and now there is a mystery surrounding their creation."

Lexie looked at Jess and Jess looked at Lexie.

"Who could have done that to our papers?" said Jess. "Perhaps there's a Phantom Painter who breaks into people's sheds and changes stuff."

"Studio," said Roland. "Not 'shed', please, Jess – and I'm sure there must be some kind of reasonable explanation."

I decided that this was the moment to let everyone see me, so I came out from behind the canvas which was hiding me, and walked across one of the pictures. It seemed

that my puddle-dipping had not
been very successful, because I left a
trail of pale pink paw-prints behind
me.

"It's Perkins!" Lexie shouted. "That's him, and he's the one who made the marks on the paper."

"Goodness!" said Wilfred. "That is truly amazing – an artistic cat! Ooh, you're a real beauty!" he said to me, and to Lexie and Jess he said: "Of course, the marks had to be made by a real cat. I can see it all now! They absolutely make the works so true, so very authentically feline! They will fit perfectly into an exhibition I am planning. I am calling it 'The Face of Nature', and these cat portraits will fit in most beautifully. The show will be mainly landscapes, of course, but these, with Perkins's own inimitable finishing touches, will be the talk of the art world. No-one will be able to resist them. I shall be in touch with the Press at once."

"What about," said Roland, "my work?" He was looking a little sad, I thought.

"Oh, divine, divine, dear chap, but not quite what I'm looking for . . . not quite *natural* enough, don't you see? I shall, however, pass your name on to one of my colleagues. I think your style is just what he may be looking for."

He swept out of the studio, and Lexie and Jess and Melissa followed him.

"I don't suppose," Roland said to me, "you'd consider taking a short walk across one of my paintings, Perkins, old chap? It might turn it into an instant masterpiece."

I fled, most eager to tell my friends in the Square what had happened, and certainly NOT wanting to dip my feet into any horrible colours ever again.

5. A Change of Plan

"Are you famous now, Perkins?"
Blossom asked me, later on Saturday
afternoon. The storm had subsided,
the sun was shining and the sky was
now a delicious pale blue.

"Perhaps not quite yet," I said,
"but I very soon will be. Mr de
Crespay has arranged for a
photographer to come and take

pictures of Lexie and Jess and myself. Of course, I will not mind that nearly as much as sitting for my portrait, because, as you know, photographs are taken so quickly. To tell you the truth, I am quite looking forward to it."

"Perhaps," said Callie wistfully, "they'll come and take a picture of you in the Square with us."

"But what about the competition?" said Geejay. "What will the girls send in now?"

I had not thought of that. I sighed. "I suppose I ought to go in and allow them to paint me again if they want to," I said. "It would hardly be fair to spoil their plans. I shall come out and see you all later."

The girls had changed their minds. When I arrived in the kitchen, they were nowhere to be seen.

"Hello, Perkins!" said Melissa. "Mr de Crespay has just left – isn't it all exciting? You are a clever cat! And the girls – aren't they talented? Mr de Crespay – I must remember to call him Wilfred – says their youthful high spirits come out in the pictures. I wonder if I have time to get my hair done before that photographer comes tomorrow? Do you want to know where the girls are? They're over at Jess's."

I was relieved to be allowed to sleep peacefully, but still I wished that Lexie and Jess had decided to stay at our house. Had they made up their minds not to enter the competition? And if they still wished to compete, how could they paint my portrait if I was not there? I fretted about this for some time, but in the end my eyes closed and I slept. In the wise words of the Furry Ancestors: "Sleep makes everything bearable."

"Perkins! Perkins, wake up!"

It was Lexie. She was standing
beside my shawl, waving a sheet of
paper in front of me. "Look at this!
Isn't it great?"

I looked. It was a painting of a
fish in a bowl.

"This is Jess's fish. He's called
Harold. We painted him this

afternoon, and we're sending his picture in to the newspaper, for the competition."

I felt a pang of jealousy, I admit it, and Lexie evidently read my mind.

"You mustn't be jealous, Perkins. You're going to be properly famous. Your pictures are going to hang in a proper gallery, and there's going to be a photo of you in the local paper.

So it's only fair that Jess's pet has his picture painted. Isn't it?"

I had to confess that it was.

6. Fame!

If you have never been famous,
permit me to tell you that it is
extremely tiring. I am not the only
cat in the Square to say this. Blossom
and Callie and Geejay shared some
of my limelight, and we all waited
with some excitement for the
newspaper to appear the next day.

While he was with us, the man with the camera never stopped talking to me, and walked around me flashing shiny lights in my eyes. He started in the house. Lexie had to cuddle me, put me on her lap, and then Jess had to do the same thing.

After that the girls had to stand and smile stupidly at sheets of paper which were pretending to be "The Perkins Paintings". They were not the real pictures, because Wilfred de Crespay had taken those off to be framed, ready to hang in his gallery.

"Kitty, kitty, kitty," the photographer kept saying, and "Over here, Pussycat . . ." and "How about a shot of you cleaning your whiskers?" and "Watch the birdy – you like watching birdies, don't you, eh?"

They took us all out to the Square in the end, because the sun was shining. Blossom, Callie and Geejay had been waiting by the railings.

"Where have you been, Perkins?"

Blossom miaowed at me, as I went to stand beside her. "We'd given up hope."

"Fabulous shot!" the photographer screeched. "Don't move a muscle, cats! Three other cats . . . the Perkins Fan Club, I bet! Stand still, kitties."

The Cuckoo Square Cats were a success. We stood and sat and looked interesting for a long time, and then at last the photographer packed his camera away and left us alone.

"You are lovely cats," Lexie said. "And if you're in the paper tomorrow, I shall come out and show you the picture."

There were two pictures in the *Bugle* the next day. One was of Lexie and Jess sitting on a Cuckoo Square bench with myself in Lexie's arms, and Blossom, Callie and Geejay gathered at the girls' feet. The other was a picture of Lexie and Jess, with yours truly looking soulful in Lexie's arms. The caption said: "Perkins, the

Pussycat Picasso!"

I explained to my friends that Picasso was a famous painter, and I think they were impressed.

"I hope," said Geejay, "that *you* won't take to wearing a velvet beret like Mr Blythe, now that you're an artist."

"Never," I said. "You know what the Furry Ancestors would say: 'East or West, fur is best'."

You will be anxious to know the results of the 'Paint Your Pet' competition. The picture of Jess's goldfish won third prize. This is, I think you will agree, an excellent result for a creature who is not a cat.

THE END